Lubaya's Quiet Roar

by Marilyn Nelson

paintings by

Philemona Williamson

Dial Books for Young Readers

Lubaya's always liked to be alone,
happily watching the theater of her thoughts.
There, she's a ballerina who talks to whales,
or an African American artist astronaut.

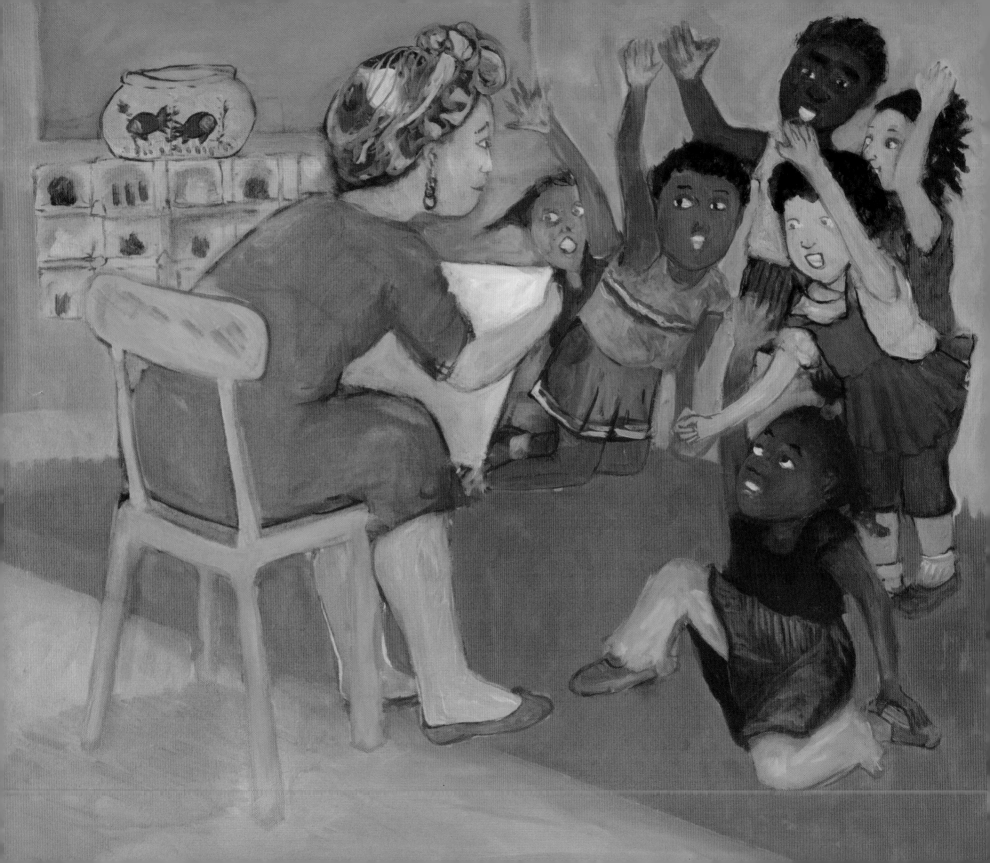

Lubaya hardly ever raises her hand,
even when she knows the right answer.
She watches the hand-waving picked kids stand
in the light of classroom admiration.

When captains choose kids to play on their teams,
Lubaya gets picked number eight or nine.
Her teammates shout "LOOBIE!" But she's lost in dreams.
She looks at the ground and shrugs when the other team wins.

At home, she notices things. The way her dad's
jaw sprouts whiskers by evening, how sometimes
he winks, and her mom's cheeks grow a brown blush.
The way her mom's eyes crinkle when she smiles.

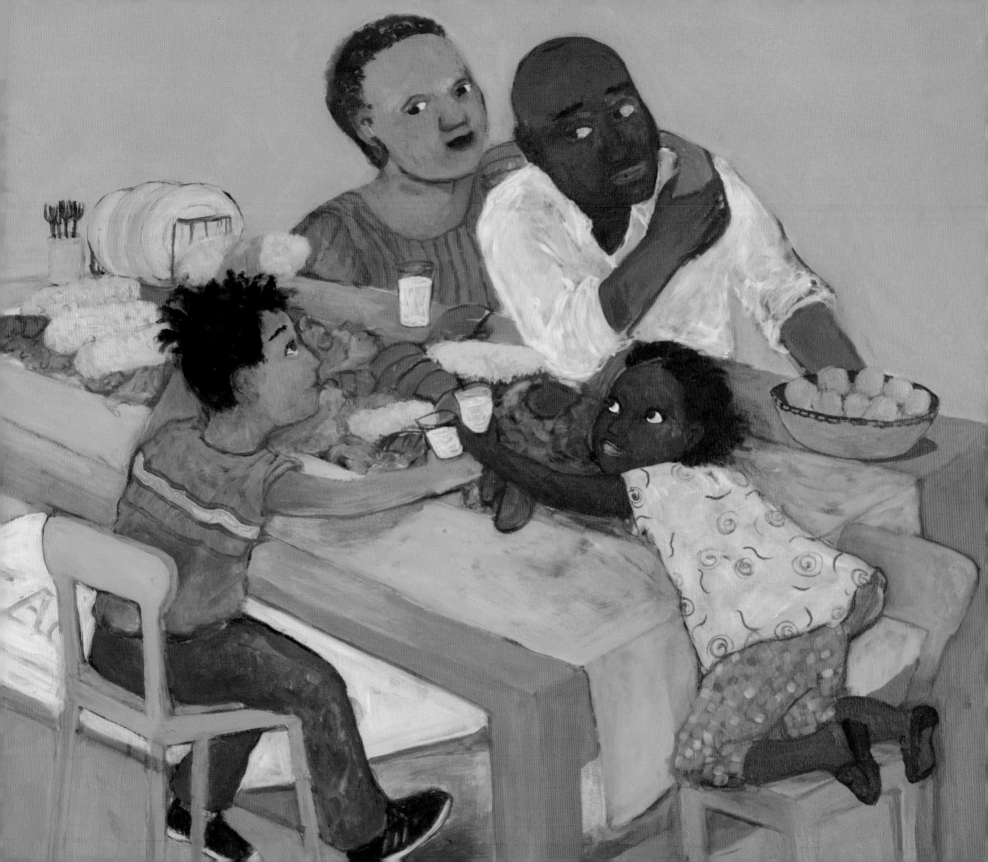